WHAT DOG KNOWS

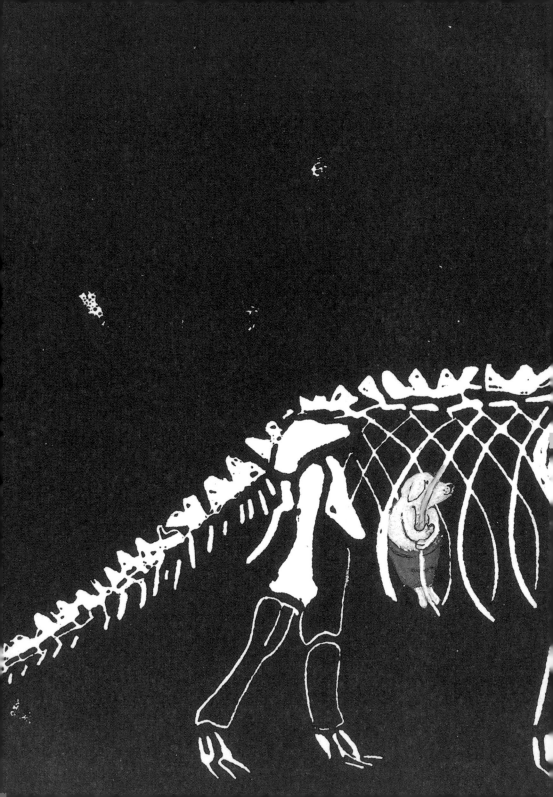

WHAT
DOG
KNOWS

Sylvia Vanden Heede
and Inge Bergh

Illustrated by
Marije Tolman

Translated by Bill Nagelkerke

For my nephew Navid
M.T.

For Rasmus and Aaron,
for Adhémar and Gust,
Louis and Damiaan,
but especially for Siem!
S.V.H.

For Florian, Matthias,
Skrolan and Killian
I.B.

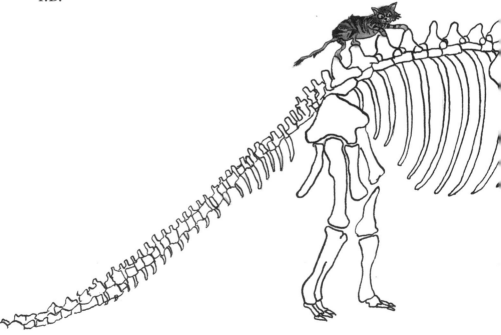

CONTENTS

MuMMies
and
SKELETONS

Wolf has a bone. "Mine!" he growls.

"That's what you think," says Dog. "It's not yours. This bone is from a cow."

"Ha ha," laughs Wolf. "What makes you think that? A cow eats grass, not bones."

That's true. A cow doesn't eat bones. Or meat. All the same, Dog is right.

This bone is from a cow.

Your body is made of flesh and blood. Inside that body are bones, which are hard. A bone is strong. It supports your body. All the bones together make up your skeleton. Without a skeleton you would be as limp as a rag.

I feel awfully limp and sick. Give me a bone, and make it quick!

TRY THIS

Life-size skeleton Lie on a big sheet of paper—the back of unused wallpaper, for example. Get someone to draw your outline with a felt-tip pen. Draw your skeleton inside the outline.

Done!

Fine! I'll add another line!

Sometimes, a bone breaks. That hurts. If you break the bone in your arm, you need to have your arm in a cast. If you break the bone in your leg, your leg has to be in a cast. The cast keeps your arm or leg still. The broken bone has a chance to grow back together.

QUIZ

What part of your skeleton can you see when you look in the mirror?

A Your hair

B Your nails

C Your teeth

A dead body is called a corpse. A corpse rots away, leaving only the bones. Snails and worms don't have bones. Neither do insects. Insects protect their soft bodies with external skeletons, called exoskeletons. These are skeletons on the outside. You can see them clearly on beetles. Their exoskeletons look like armor.

These bones look very fishy.

I scratch the black; the white comes back. How cool is that?

TRY THIS

Scratch drawing Paint a sheet of white cardboard with black poster paint. (Hint: add some liquid soap to the paint first.) Leave it to dry. With the tip of some craft scissors scratch the skeleton of a fish onto the paint. The white underneath will reappear.

Done!

"I know something I didn't know before," says Dog. "I read it in a book. There's a bone in my ear."

"A bone in your ear?" cries Wolf. "Come and let me pull it out!"

Wolf is already licking his lips. But that's ridiculous because the bone can't come out.

It's deep inside and tiny. As small as a D. It's shaped like a D as well. It looks just like a D written backwards!

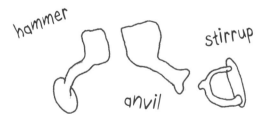

Wolf looks disappointed. A tiny bone is no good to him. One bite, one swallow, and it would be gone.

Wolf sighs: "It doesn't even look like a bone. It looks more like…more like…"

Oh dear, Wolf doesn't know his ABCs. Or his D. Bad luck!

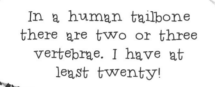

In a human tailbone there are two or three vertebrae. I have at least twenty!

A person has more than two hundred bones. The longest bone in your body is the thigh bone. The smallest bones are the stirrup, the anvil, and the hammer. You need these tiny bones for hearing. They are deep inside your ear.

Touch your ear. Is it bony? No, it's made of cartilage. Cartilage is hard yet bendy. That's handy. It means your ear doesn't break when you lie on it. There's also cartilage in your nose and inside your body—where two bones meet, for example. When you were younger, you had more cartilage. As you grow older, some of this cartilage hardens and turns into real bone. Your wrist bones don't fully harden until you are a teenager. You can tell a child's age from the amount of cartilage in their skeleton.

My ear's crackling!

There's something Dog doesn't understand.

"What is it? What?" growls Wolf. "Something about a bone? I'll know the answer. You think I'm stupid? Go ahead and ask!"

Dog looks at Wolf. Could Wolf really know? That would be great!

"How is a bone attached?" Dog asks.

'Um…' says Wolf. He scratches his head. "Attached to what?

To an animal? Or a piece of meat?
To a muscle or sinew? What a treat!

Ha, that rhymes!" Wolf laughs. He loves rhyme.

But Dog is none the wiser. "To another bone," he explains. "How is one bone attached to another? And how does a leg bend?"

"Ha ha!" laughs Wolf.

*"With four legs and a bone,
I can take my dinner home!*

Nice—another rhyme!"
Dog stops asking questions. Wolf
is being silly.
"I'll look it up in a book," Dog says.
Wolf replies:

*"Look it up in a book?
That's how people learn to cook!"*

Your bones are connected to one another. Some bones
can't move, such as the bones of your skull. When you
were born, they hadn't grown together—that happened
later. Together those bones in your skull make a kind of
helmet, which protects your brain.

Other bones move a little. Put your hand on your chest and take a deep breath. Can you feel your chest expand? Between your ribs and your breastbone is a piece of cartilage. This cartilage makes sure that your ribs can move to give your lungs enough room to breathe.

Try scratching your nose without bending your arm. Or riding a bicycle with straight legs. Can you? Of course not! That's why you need elbows and knees, which are joints. Your arm bones meet at the elbow. Your leg bones meet at the knee. There are joints in your fingers, toes, ankles, wrists, hips, and shoulders, too. Even in your neck! Try them out and see.

In each joint there is fluid, surrounded by cartilage. The fluid is as thick as egg white. It lets the joint move smoothly. The cartilage protects the ends of the bones.

There are strong bands around each joint. Not hair bands! Not musical bands! The bands around your joints are called ligaments. Ligaments connect bones to other bones.

Dog snaps the book shut. He stretches
a leg. He flexes a toe.

"Have you finished the book?"
asks Wolf.

"No," says Dog. "Not yet.

But the more I read, the more I know.
And that's the only way to go."

"It also helps the rhymes to flow,"
laughs Wolf.

QUIZ

What's in your skull?

A   Your lungs

B   Your brain

C   Your intestines

Nothing

Where's Wolf slinking off to?
But is it really Wolf? He looks so
strange wrapped in white from top
to toe. Is he in a plaster cast?
Has he broken his foot?
And his head? And his back
and belly and tail? Surely not!

"Shush!" hisses Wolf.
"Shush!" He doesn't want
Dog to hear or see him yet.
Wolf wants to play a trick
on him.

Dog is sitting in his
chair reading the
paper. "Boo!" he
suddenly hears.
And there's Wolf!
"Boo!" Wolf
shouts again.

23

But Dog doesn't get a fright. He folds
up the paper. "Hi there, Wolf," he says.
"Nice of you to drop by. I'm ready for
a cup of tea. Would you like one?"

"Boo, heurghh!" Wolf makes an eerie
growl. "I'm not Wolf. I'm a mummy.
And I don't drink tea, only blood. Boo,
hiss, heurghh!"

Dog laughs. "Boo who?" he says.
"A mummy doesn't drink blood.
It doesn't drink anything because
a mummy's dead."

"Dead?"

"Yes. As dead as a
doornail. A mummy
is a dead body. Didn't
you know that?"

Wolf says nothing.
He's disappointed.
Dog wasn't scared.
That's no fun!

"Give me some tea
then," he growls.

And Dog does that. But the tea is very hot.

"Oww!" cries Wolf. He's burnt his tongue. And his snout. And his paw. Now he really needs bandages—just like a mummy!

A dead body rots. That happens naturally. That's why a dead body is buried or cremated. You can't keep a body forever. Not unless it's turned into a mummy! Because a mummy is a dead body that doesn't decay.

It's possible to make a mummy. That's what the Ancient Egyptians did. Most of Egypt is desert, which is good for preserving dead bodies. The hot sand dried them out and they shrank, a little like raisins. Then they couldn't rot. For something to rot, moisture is needed. Later, the Egyptians made mummies another way. They dried their dead themselves using herbs, salt, resin, and spices.

Making a mummy was complicated. Not just anyone was allowed to do it. Priests carried out special rituals, and everything had to be done correctly.

Mummies of very rich people were sometimes placed in three coffins, one inside the other. A pharaoh (a king) was given a huge tomb: a pyramid. Many of these pyramids are still standing today. Less wealthy people were buried in simple graves. And the poor went on being buried in the sand.

You can keep a raisin for a long time, but not a grape.

But, very rich or very poor, everyone wanted their body to be preserved as well as possible. The Egyptians believed you couldn't exist in the afterlife without a body.

It wasn't only people that were mummified. Animals were, too. Underground tunnels have been discovered in Egypt, full of mummified dogs. The dogs were offerings to Anubis, the god of the dead who has the head of a jackal. A jackal looks a little like a dog, so he received the gift of dead dogs. What about cats? Yes, they were offered as well, to the cat goddess, Bastet. Thousands of cat mummies have been discovered. Some were house cats that died naturally. But most were killed on purpose. You can see that from their mummies.

QUIZ

What is a mummy?

A   A dead body that won't rot

B   A dead body that drinks blood

C   A living body

TRY THIS

Dried apple slices Peel and core an apple. Cut the apple into thin slices. Dip the slices into a small bowl of water (about two cups) with a teaspoon of salt dissolved in it. Drain. Dry the slices for two hours in a very low oven (70°C / 160°F), leaving the door slightly open if possible. Take the slices out of the oven and let them dry for another hour.

Done!

Every salty sprinkle adds another wrinkle.

Wolf is up to something.

He ties on an apron and puts on a hat. Now he looks like a chef. That's very odd because Wolf never cooks. He eats his meat raw, which saves a lot of work.

Dog comes along.

"Ha, good timing!" Wolf growls. "Lend me a paw. Pass me that knife."

Dog looks up in surprise. Wolf in an apron and hat! That's a new sight.

He picks up the knife and passes it to Wolf.

"What are you cooking?" Dog asks.

"I'm not cooking anything. I'm preparing something," Wolf snaps. "Can't you tell?"

Dog scratches his head. "Oh," he says. "What are you preparing?"

Wolf curls his lip. He looks very scary. Dog is scared. That knife is sharp!

"Look out! Don't cut me. I'm your cousin," Dog says quickly. "You can cut leeks, chop onions, make soup, or bake a cake. But don't hurt me!"

The knife flashes. Wolf's glance is just as sharp. "Bah, soup!" he cries. "Soup is green! And I hate green! Didn't you know that? I don't chop onions and I don't bake cakes. Don't be such a scaredy-dog. I'm not going to hurt you. I'm making…making…I'm making something with Cat!"

Dog lets out a yelp. He feels faint. "Cat!" he cries. "Is Cat dead? Are you going to eat her? You can't! You mustn't! That would be murder!"

Wolf laughs loudly. His teeth are so sharp. His jaws are cavernous.

"Ha, ha," laughs Wolf. "I'm not going to eat Cat. How could I? That creature would taste foul. Raw or cooked, well done or rare. No, I'm not going to fry or bake her.

I'm going to make her into
a mummy. It'll be great fun."
  The knife flashes again.

Dog swallows. His throat is dry.
  He breaks out in a sweat.
  "A…a mummy?" he asks faintly.

"Do you mean that, Wolf? Or are you joking? Oh, I get it… You're not really making a mummy, are you? You're only teasing, right? Just like before, when you called out 'Boo!' and I didn't get a fright. Is that it, Wolf?"

Wolf smirks and sharpens the knife. "Read out loud, Dog. Read from that book. Yes, that one lying there. It explains how it's done."

"How what's done?" asks Dog.

"What I have to do with Cat," says Wolf as he sharpens the knife again.

RECIPE FOR A MUMMY
(according to Wolf)

1. Wash the dead body with oil or water.

2. Empty the head and stomach.

3. Do the same with the chest, but leave the heart in place.

4. Soak the liver, stomach, lungs, and intestines in pots of salt.

5. Stuff the stomach and chest with spices and salt.

6. Dry the body in salt.

7. Leave it for 40-70 days.

8. Remove the body from the salt and wash it out in a bath. Caution! Use preservative rather than soap.

9. Take the body out of the bath and dry it. Fill it with sawdust. Rub it with oil. Pour resin over it.

10. Wrap the body many times in strips of cloth.

11. Place the mummy in the coffin of your choice.

Wolf tests the knife. He feels how sharp it is now.

"Perfect!" he crows. "This knife is as sharp as…as, ah…a knife. Cat's in for it now. Slash! I'll slice her stomach. Slash! Out it comes. Slash!"

The knife flashes and glints.

Dog feels sick. He turns pale, completely pale. He covers his eyes.

"What's the matter, Dog? Are you ill or something? Don't throw up on my floor. Go outside and get some fresh air. And if you see Cat, grab her! Yes, it's time to bring her in."

Now Dog understands.

Wolf's scared of Cat. And Cat's scared of Dog. So Wolf wants Dog to catch Cat.

But Dog won't. How could he? "Catch Cat yourself!" he says.

Wolf looks sour.

Dog doesn't want to and Wolf doesn't dare to! He'll never catch Cat.

"And I wanted a mummy so badly…" he sulks.

Poor Wolf.

But suddenly he laughs again. "I know," he says. "I'll make a mummy out of Bear."

"Out of Bear? My bear?"

Wolf nods. "He's already lost his voice. He won't have to lose that again, which makes it easier. And do you know the best thing? Bear doesn't bite or scratch. He doesn't hiss or spit. Give me your bear, Dog. Quick! So I can get to work!"

Dog steps back, trembling. "No!" he begs.
"Don't do that, Wolf. Wait, I'll think of
something else. Ha, I have an idea already.
Give me your apron, hat, and knife."

Dog puts on the hat and ties on the
apron. And this is what he does:

TRY THIS

A mummy roll Roll a sausage in puff pastry. Leave one end of the sausage sticking out for the face. Bake for fifteen minutes in a hot oven (225°C / 440°F). Allow to cool. Make two small eyes on the "face" with mayonnaise, mustard, or sauce.

Done!

Egyptian mummies are famous, but mummies have been found elsewhere, too. Even at the North Pole. Because a dead body in ice doesn't rot. It stays as fresh as meat in the freezer. The body becomes an ice-mummy.

QUIZ

What is an ice-mummy?

A A mummy shaped like an ice-block

B An ice-block shaped like a mummy

C A mummy made by freezing

"Dog! Dog! Dog! Help! Dog! Dog!"
howls Wolf.

Dog can hear his cousin from a long
way away. He leaps from his basket.

"I'm coming, Wolf!" he calls. "Hang
on! I'll save you!"

Dog runs as fast as he can. His cousin
needs him! Has his house collapsed?
Did a tree fall on the roof? Is the forest
on fire? Or did Cat come?

It's all the same to Dog. He'd go
through fire for his cousin!

"Wolf...Wolf..." Dog puffs.

Wolf is lying idly in the grass, gnawing
a bone. Then he sees Dog.

He grins and burps. He sighs: "Ha,
there you are. I've been calling for
ages. What took you so long? It's such
a mess around here, I can't stand it.

So I thought, I'll call Dog to help me.
He'll tidy things up."

Dog pants. His tongue hangs out and
he clutches his chest. That kind of hurry
is bad for his heart. And Wolf doesn't
even need him! Cat hasn't attacked him.
His house is in one piece. There's not a
single tree on fire.

"What...what...what..." wheezes Dog.
That's all he can get out. He gasps for air.
   "What, what, what?" growls Wolf.
"Can't you see there's stuff everywhere?
Jump to it!"
   Wolf throws the bone at Dog.
   But Dog ducks in time. Missed, Wolf!
   "Get a bag. Throw the mess in and
take the bag to your boss. He'll know
what to do with it."

Dog turns livid. He's so angry! He barks:
"Do your own dirty work. I'm not lifting

a paw to help. I'm not your slave. I'm not a robot either. You're just a lazy-bones."

Wolf leaps up. "What did you say about a bone? Did you bring one? Is it big? Hand it over! I want that bone!"

Wolf doesn't listen.

"I said you're a lazy-bones," Dog repeats. "And I'm not your robot."

Wolf doesn't even know what a robot is.

So Dog explains.

"A robot is a thing made of steel or tin. Or this and that. Sometimes it looks like a person or an animal. But it's not alive. It doesn't feel or think like a person. A robot works. That's what it's made to do."

Dog explains it all carefully. Then he explains it again. And again and again and again. Until Wolf gets it.

The word "robot" comes from "robota," which is Czech for "forced to work." Robots make our life easier by doing difficult or heavy jobs. A robot's work is very precise.

QUIZ

What does "robota" mean?

A To make robots

B To do nothing

C To be forced to work

A robot is a machine, but not just any machine. Many machines do only one thing. A cutting machine cuts material into pieces. A sewing machine sews the pieces together. A robot can do both. It also vacuums up the fluff!

Robots are often found in factories. They never get tired. They don't complain and they don't go on strike. They can be extremely precise, which is pretty handy.

Robots also do dangerous work. They clear up mines
and bombs. They check out areas where the air might be
toxic to people. They even drive around on the moon.
Or dive deep into the sea. People could die doing
those things. But a robot is never afraid. After all, it
doesn't feel anything. It's only an object.

That's not so in movies where robots often look like people with a head and arms. And claws instead of hands. They're happy, angry, or sad. They even fall in love!

Sometimes it seems that robots can think like us. But that's not yet possible. There's a computer inside controlling the robot.

TRY THIS

Marshmallow robot Push a marshmallow onto the end of a skewer. Dip the marshmallow into melted chocolate. Leave the chocolate to firm up a little. Before it is completely dry, stick on rings from a candy necklace as eyes and two gum drops or smaller pieces of chocolate on the side for ears. Use licorice to make a mouth.

Done!

If I hold the bag just so, I can gulp them down in just one go!

Wolf puts on a pair of glasses and picks up a fat book from the library. He looks inside.

He turns a page. And the next, and the next.

Dog turns up. He can't believe his eyes. "Are you reading, Wolf? I didn't think you could!"

Wolf laughs and boasts: "I've been able to read for ages! But I'd lost my glasses and now I've found them."

Wolf taps his glasses. He looks so intelligent.

"Just you wait, Dog," he says. "When I've finished this book I'll know more than you."

"But..." says Dog.

Wolf raises his paw. "Quiet! Don't interrupt when I'm reading."

Dog finds it a bit strange. Wolf with a book? What sort of book is it? Does it have lots of words and is Wolf actually reading them? Surely not.

"Finished!" says Wolf. He slams the book shut and takes off his glasses with a grin. "Go on, ask me a question," he says.

Dog scratches his ear. "What kind of question?"

Wolf sighs. "A question like:

—How does a robot fight?
—What does a robot eat?
—Where does a robot live?"

"But that's nonsense," Dog cries. "A robot doesn't eat or have a house."

"No?" growls Wolf. "That's what it says in this book. Read it yourself. You might learn something."

Dog takes the book. "Oh, Wolf," he laughs. "You weren't reading. You were just looking! What's on the cover?"

"A robot," growls Wolf. "A robot with a sword."

"No," says Dog. "It only looks like one. It's not a robot, but a knight in a suit of steel. But he's a flesh and blood person."

Wolf licks his lips.

"Flesh and blood is food and drink.
That, dear cousin, is what I think.

And it rhymes as well!"

Knights lived in the Middle Ages, around one thousand years ago. A knight fought in the service of a lord. His job was to fight. A knight was more than a soldier. He was a warrior on horseback. His charger, or war-horse, was strong and courageous. And very expensive. But that didn't matter because a knight was well rewarded for fighting.

QUIZ

What is a charger?

A A rusty weapon

B A war-horse

C A stubborn ox

If the lord won a battle he gave his knights money and horses. Sometimes a knight even received land and a house. Or a wife! That way the knight became wealthy, too.

In fact, after a while everyone wanted to become a knight. Poets composed wonderful stories about knights. They made up adventures and wrote them down. Have you heard of King Arthur and the Knights of the Round Table? They probably never existed. But knights of the Middle Ages wanted to be like them.

A knight had to always behave well. It was called being "chivalrous." A real knight was pious, which meant he tried to live a good Christian life. Courage, strength, and loyalty were very important. A knight was not allowed to lie or steal or cheat anyone. He shared what he had and protected the weak.

You couldn't simply become a knight. You started off as a page and then became a squire, which is a knight's assistant. Every knight had one. A squire looked after the charger and groomed it. He polished the weapons, helmet, and chain mail, and carried the shield. He did everything the knight asked.

"Ha!" cried Wolf. "Now I get it! A knight isn't a robot, but a squire is. Because he does whatever the knight asks. He doesn't complain or go on strike. Isn't that right?"

Dog shakes his head. "A squire is alive. He thinks and feels. He gets tired, and he grows up. A robot can't do that."

It's true what Dog says. A squire doesn't stay a squire. One day he will be grown up.

And then...and then... What then?
Read on!

It takes a long time to become a knight. You start when you're about seven. Then you become a page. You no longer live with your parents but instead with another noble family in a castle. You help the knights and wait on the ladies. And you have time to learn many things. Reading and writing are not usually among them. What do you learn? Good manners. And you have riding lessons. That sounds like fun.

You can't become a squire until you turn fourteen. Every squire serves his own knight. He learns archery, wrestling, lance-throwing, sword-fighting, and much more. Sometimes a squire takes part in a war or a pitched battle. But usually he does all the boring jobs, just like a robot. So Wolf is right about that.

A page is always a boy. No girls allowed. Silly, eh?

Are you twenty-one? And have you passed all your tests? Then the big day is almost here. First there's a long night to endure when you mustn't sleep or talk.

You pray all night long. You won't be knighted until the next morning. Then you receive your own sword…and your own squire!

Being knighted doesn't hurt. The squire kneels before his lord and bows his head. The lord gives him a tap on the shoulder—with his sword. But it's a gentle tap. And the lord doesn't use the sharp edge of the sword, otherwise knighthood could be fatal!

Ow!

QUIZ

What does "being knighted" mean?

A   A fight between knights

B   A tap on the shoulder with a sword

C   A blow from a knight's sword

"Fine, fine," growls Wolf. "A squire isn't a robot because a squire grows up. And a knight isn't a robot either because he used to be a squire. Then he got tapped on the shoulder, which made him a knight. A knight of flesh and blood. Canned flesh and blood! Mmm!"

Wolf drools. He's so hungry!

Dog says quickly: "You're wrong, Wolf. Armor isn't made of soft metal. As I told you, it's made of iron or steel, which are hard. Very hard. Honestly, your teeth wouldn't make a dent."

Tough luck for Wolf. He could almost taste that knight!

A knight's armor was very heavy—it could weigh as much as he did! When a knight fell, he needed help to get back onto his feet. It was very awkward to mount a horse, too, wearing all that metal. Sometimes a knight was tired out before the battle began.

Horses also wore armor to protect them in battle. That's why a war-horse had to be big and strong. It was more like a farm horse than a racehorse. A knight and horse both clothed in metal looked a bit like a tank. If they charged, it was best to get out of the way.

Knights also fought each other for sport, holding jousts or tournaments. These were pretty dangerous. There were always injuries and often deaths, but the tournament went on regardless. The winners received a lot of money, weapons, and horses. That's how some poor knights quickly became rich.

TRY THIS

Sword and shield Cut a sword shape out of cardboard. Cover it with tin foil. Use the lid of a cooking pot as a shield.

Done!

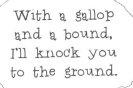

With a gallop and a bound, I'll knock you to the ground.

Dog has a patch around one eye. Wolf doesn't.

"That patch of yours is peculiar," scoffs Wolf. "It covers your eye."

Dog doesn't mind. A patch is perfect. "I used to be a pirate," he says, "with a ship and treasure. I lost them both. But I still have the patch to prove it."

Dog is lying. He wasn't a pirate.

But Wolf falls for it, hook, line, and sinker. "Treasure?" he drools. "Treasure with real gold and lots of money? You were rich, Dog!"

"Very rich," Dog nods. "As rich as the sea is deep. And that's very deep."

Dog laughs to himself. Oh, Wolf! It's only a joke. But Wolf can't see it.

Close your eyes and think of a pirate. What do you see? A black flag with skull and crossbones? A captain with a peg leg and a hook instead of a hand? With an eye-patch and parrot? Do you see an old wooden ship and smoking cannons? Powder kegs and barrels of rum? And a ship's hold full of gold and jewels? That's not surprising. We know pirates from movies and books. They drink a lot, shoot all the time, sing loudly, raid other ships, steal gold and jewels, and bury their treasure in the sand. In real life, it wasn't quite like that.

Wolf looks disappointed. "It's sad, so sad," he moans.

"What's so sad?" asks Dog.

"That the treasure's lost," cries Wolf. "I've been thinking about that money, day and night. I'm your cousin, Dog. I'm entitled to half of it! In fact, more, because I'm Wolf. I grab whatever I can and that's just the way it is."

Wolf is really upset but Dog can't help himself. He holds his paw over his mouth so Wolf can't see him laughing. Dog pretends to be thinking. He sighs and frowns and stares into space.

"What is it, Dog? What can you see?" asks Wolf. He also stares into space.

"I was thinking about the map," says Dog.

"The map?" says Wolf.

Dog nods. "Yes. A map with an X."

Wolf leaps up. "A map with an X. Why didn't you say so? Give me the map, Dog, so I can find the treasure. I know how to do it."

"So do I," says Dog. "It's easy: Find the spot marked by the X. Dig a hole. And there's the treasure."

"What are you waiting for? Dig, Dog, dig!" Wolf yells.

"There's just one small problem," says Dog. "The map's gone missing. So we can't do anything."

Wolf is wild. He snarls and growls. He'll bite Dog any minute. Dog is his cousin but that means nothing to Wolf. He bites whoever he feels like biting.

Dog is scared. He says quickly: "Oh, now I remember! I know where the map might be. Wait here, Wolf, and I'll fetch it. I won't be long."

Pirates are sea robbers, bandits with boats. They raid other ships and steal the cargo. Or sometimes the whole ship.

Pirating is old, as old as seafaring itself. But its heyday began in the 16th century. Ships laden with goods sailed between Europe, Africa, and America. Pirates hid away in caves and on deserted islands to wait for a ship to come by. Then they sent their own ship after it. They sold the stolen goods, or kept them for their own use.

And what about the treasure? There probably wasn't any buried treasure. Or hardly any. Those stories came later. The famous book *Treasure Island* by Robert Louis Stevenson wasn't written until 1883. Long John Silver, one of the main characters, was a one-legged pirate with a parrot on his shoulder. Since then, we imagine pirates looking like him. And buried treasure goes with it.

Dog is home. He doesn't have a map and there's no treasure! But he thinks, I'll play a trick on my cousin.

Guess what Dog does. He draws his own map, a complete fake. But it looks just like the real thing!

Girls couldn't be knights. But they could be pirates!

TRY THIS

Treasure map Crumple up a sheet of white paper. Smooth it out. Wipe it with a used teabag. Leave the paper to dry. Draw your own map of where the treasure is hidden.

Done!

Seafarers need to be able to see a long distance. Otherwise they won't spot an approaching ship until too late. Or they'll accidentally sail past an island.

The higher you are, the further you can see. The highest place on a ship is the top of the mast so the crow's nest goes there. It's not actually the nest of a crow. It's a lookout spot.

When Dog finds the spot, I'll take the lot!

In piratical times the crow's nest was called a "basket," which it actually was—the sort of large, deep basket roving traders or peddlers carried on their back. The name "crow's nest" came much later when there were no longer as many sailing ships. They had been replaced by steam ships, and the pirates' "basket" was now a steel platform with a rail. From a distance it looked like a nest of branches. The platform hung just below the funnel so the lookout got soot on his nice clothes. If he wore black instead, the soot didn't show. But now he looked like a crow, which, of course, is also black.

QUIZ

What is a crow's nest?

A   A ball of rope

B   A messy cabin

C   A lookout post

Privateers were a particular kind of pirate. They received a letter of commission from the king. The letter commanded them to capture enemy ships, so that was their duty. Privateers were not allowed to keep the spoils, but the king rewarded them well.

Privateers were very handy in times of war. In those days there were no planes or missiles. A war was often fought at sea, which is why battleships were built. They carried rows of cannons.

Cargo ships had to keep an eye out for privateers, as well.

Pirates captured a ship by boarding it, which meant climbing onto a ship without consent. First, the pirates threw ropes with grappling hooks at the ship. They used these to pull their own ship closer. Sometimes they laid planks from one ship to the other, then they climbed quickly aboard and plundered what they could. Sometimes they took over the ship itself. As for the crew, more often than not, they lost their lives.

Pirates aren't the only people who board ships. So do the police. But not to steal, rob, or plunder!

Police board a ship to make sure all is as it should be: that the paperwork is in order, that the captain has paid the correct fees, and that there are no drugs or smuggled goods on board. Police don't board with grappling hooks and ropes. And they don't do away with the crew. Thank goodness for that!

QUIZ

What is boarding?

A Climbing on board a ship

B Surfing

C Coating a ship's timbers with tar

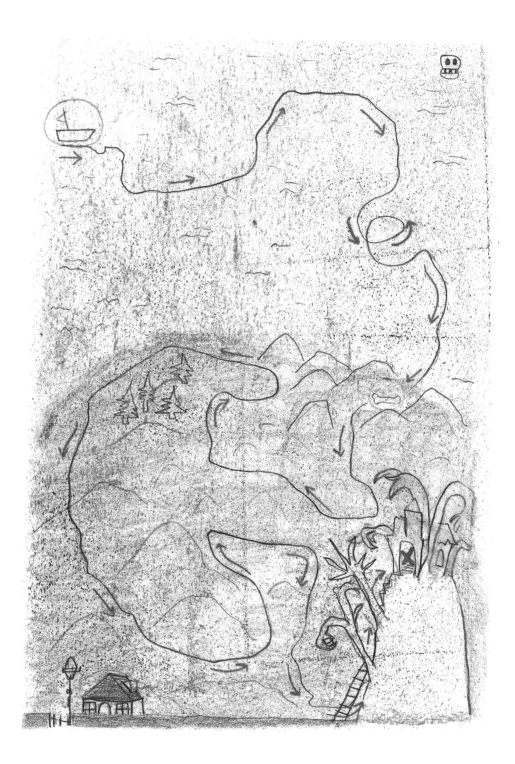

"Here's the map," says Dog.

Wolf looks at it. He scratches his head and growls: "That looks like my forest. And there's my house."

"Mm-hmm," nods Dog. He keeps his mouth clamped shut so the laugh can't escape!

Wolf doesn't notice anything. "Is the treasure here?" he asks. "Right at my door?"

"Mm-hmm," Dog nods again.

But, uh-oh, he can't stop the laugh! It bursts out.

"Ha, ha, Wolf! I fooled you! There's no treasure because I never was a pirate. And my patch is just a mark."

Wolf curls his lip and growls, "I can see right through you, Dog. You don't want me to find the treasure so you tell me whatever you want to. You can't fool me. Pick up the spade and dig a hole. Dig, Dog. Dig!"

Poor Dog! But he has no choice because "once a wolf, always a wolf." Wolf bites when he's angry. And now he's very angry.

"Dig, Dog. Dig! Dig!"

Pirates still exist today. They operate mainly out of Africa and Asia. Modern pirates are very dangerous. They prefer to attack tankers, which is easy because tankers travel slowly. They steal the tanker's safe or they take the crew captive and free them only in exchange for ransom. But sometimes the pirates want the whole ship. They kill the crew so they won't cause any trouble. Then they repaint the tanker, falsify the papers, give the ship another name, and sell it for a lot of money. The police and navies throughout the world hunt for these pirates but they're hard to capture.

dinosaurs
and
dragons

In front of Wolf's house is a very deep hole.

"Dog! Dog!" Wolf calls down the hole.

"Og! Og!" he hears.

But that's not Dog. That's Wolf's voice echoing. That's what happens with a deep hole.

Dog's in the hole. He's no longer white. He's black with dirt. His back hurts and his tongue's hanging out.

"Oh, Wolf," he whimpers. "Wolf, this is pointless! There's no treasure. I was tricking you. Really, truly."

Wolf can't hear Dog. He calls: "Have you found anything? Can you feel the treasure chest or see the money?"

Dog sinks to the ground. He looks up at the light far above. He wants to be there. He wants to be out of this hole.

"Please, Wolf, please," Dog begs.

But Wolf yells: "Dig! Dig!"

"Ig! Ig!" calls the hole.

Dog picks up the spade and digs a little more. It's slow work. But suddenly...

Thud!

"What could that be?" wonders Dog. "Is there treasure here after all? But there can't be. The map was a fake!"

Thud!

There's something in the ground. A stone? A piece of rock? A...a...Dog badly wants to see what it is. But it's dark. Dog feels with his paw, along one side and then the other... And yes, he knows what it is.

"A bone!" Dog cheers. "And what a bone. It's the bone of a giant!"

The earth has many layers. The deeper you dig, the older the layer. Each layer is different, made up of things left behind by time: stones and shells. Fossils, too. Fossils are the remains of animals and plants from long ago. They are petrified—turned to stone.

Do you remember what happens when a creature dies? The flesh decomposes, or rots away, but bones last longer. Sometimes for millions of years! How can that be?

If a dead body lies underwater, the skeleton sinks into the mud where there's little oxygen. That means the skeleton can't rot away. The mud hardens into rock over thousands of years, and the bones become part of the rock. In other words, they become petrified, or fossilized.

There are also fossils that show what the whole animal looked like, not just its skeleton. That's possible when the body has left an imprint in the hardening rock.

The animal itself decomposes but the imprint remains. That's how even fossilized footprints of dinosaurs survived.

Some people used to think that the fossilized bones of dinosaurs really belonged to giants. In China these fossils were thought to be the bones of dragons. People believed the bones had the power to heal.

Not until the 19th century did scientists realize that the giant bones belonged to extinct reptiles. In 1842 these extinct reptiles were all named "dinosaurs," which means "terrible lizards."

QUIZ

What is a fossil?

A   An old dragon

B   A petrified relic

C   A dragon-stone

How do you know how old a fossil is? By testing the radioactivity of the fossil and by looking at the layer in the ground where it was found. The deeper the layer, the further back in time you go, but only if the layers of earth or rock haven't been disturbed.

"You didn't find treasure but a bone's not bad," growls Wolf.

The huge bone is lying in the grass. It's twice the size of Wolf!

Dog dug it up. It was such hard work he can hardly lift a paw. He lies down in the grass beside the bone.

"You're welcome to have a gnaw," says Wolf. "That bone's too big for me. I'll never finish it."

That's kind of Wolf. But Dog isn't hungry. He's far too tired. In the wink of an eye, he's asleep.

Wolf growls: "That's great! For once, I'm sharing, and he doesn't want any. Fine. I'll eat it by myself." He bites into the bone.

Clunk!

"Ow!" shrieks Wolf. "My tooth! My tooth!"

"What's wrong with your tooth?" asks Dog. He's not asleep now. Wolf's making too much noise.

"My tooth hurts! That bone's made of a stone. Is that another one of your tricks, Dog? Did you bury a stone bone to fool me? Bah! Some joke! It's not even funny."

But Dog had nothing to do with it.

He examines the bone. It's so big and was buried so deep. It must be very, very old. So old, it turned to stone.

Dog ponders. The bone is from a gigantic animal that's been dead a long time. A very, very, very long time, because it was buried so far down.

And then Dog realizes.

"This is a dinosaur bone," says Dog.

There were many different kinds of dinosaur living millions of years ago, long before there were people on Earth. All of them are now extinct.

You're sure to have heard of these three dinosaurs: Tyrannosaurus Rex (T-rex to its friends) was a meat-eater with a body as long as a bus. Its head was as long as your body. And its teeth? Each one was as big as your hand.

T-rex lived in the same period as Triceratops, roughly 67 million years ago in the "Cretaceous" period. Cretaceous comes from "creta," the Latin word for "chalk."

Triceratops looked very dangerous! But it wasn't a predator. It ate plants and used its horns to defend itself from enemies like T-rex. T-rex enjoyed a mouthful of Triceratops, but it wasn't easy to kill one. Triceratops was about three times as big and heavy as a rhinoceros. It also looked a bit like one.

Stegosaurus was also a plant-eater. It lived in the Jurassic period, around 150 million years ago—even earlier than the Cretaceous period. So T-rex and Triceratops never met Stegosaurus. No one knows why Stegosaurus had such large, bony plates on its back. Were they used to attract a mate? Or to cool it down when it got too hot? Maybe one day you'll discover the answer to this question!

QUIZ

What is a T-rex?

A   A dinosaur that ate plants

B   A dinosaur that ate fish

C   A dinosaur that ate meat

"Ha, ah, um…a dinosaur. I know what that is," says Wolf. "It's a dragon."

But Wolf has that wrong because a dragon isn't real.

"A dragon is an animal out of a book. It breathes fire, which dinosaurs don't do," says Dog.

"How do you know?" asks Wolf.

"I read it," says Dog.

"In a book?" asks Wolf, craftily.

Dog nods.

Wolf laughs.

"Have you ever seen a dinosaur, Dog? Here, in the forest or at home, with your boss? Or in the zoo?"

Dog shakes his head and Wolf laughs even harder.

"Then a dinosaur isn't real either. It's out of a book, just like a dragon. True or not?"

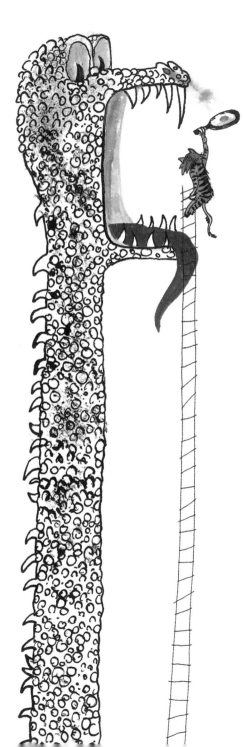

"Not true," says Dog. "I've never seen a dinosaur. No one has. There haven't been any dinosaurs for a long time, but the bones are still there."

Dog points to the gigantic bone. "Did you bite into thin air before, Wolf? Or into a bone out of a book?"

"Grr…" says Wolf, staring at the bone. He shakes his head and touches his tooth. It still hurts. And the pain is definitely real!

Fossil footprint Mix a cup of white flour with a cup of salt and some water. Stir in four tablespoons of coffee grounds. Shape two bones from this mixture or make an impression of a dinosaur's footprint. Leave overnight to dry.

Done!

> The dinosaur is dead but I have its leg!

Complete dinosaur skeletons are hardly ever found. Usually just a few loose bones or teeth turn up, or a single claw. People who put dinosaur skeletons together have to love puzzles.

No one has ever found a dragon's bone, not even a small one, because a dragon is not a dinosaur. Dragons might look a bit like dinosaurs but they never existed. They only appear in stories.

Dragons have scales, like snakes or crocodiles, and most have bat-like wings. Dragons' feet have sharp claws and a dragon's breath is burning hot—nearly all of them breathe fire. Some have more than one head.

QUIZ

What is a dragon?

A   A dinosaur with wings

B   A creature out of a book

C   A dinosaur that breathes fire

Look around in a Chinese restaurant. You'll see dragons everywhere. They bring light and good luck. A Chinese dragon has a magical pearl in its beard, which the dragon protects. The dragon also protects people from harm.

European dragons are ugly and dangerous. Whoever slays a dragon is a hero.

QUIZ

What does a dragon have?

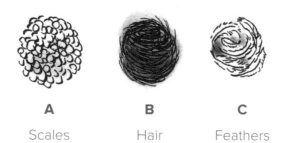

A   **B**   **C**

Scales   Hair   Feathers

So a dragon resembles a dinosaur, but do all dinosaurs look like dragons? Not at all! There were many different kinds of dinosaurs. Gigantic plant-eaters such as Diplodocus looked like a long bridge. Others looked more like chickens. Truly! Some with feathers on their tails and feet could even fly a little, but not high in the air. However, some reptiles really could fly. They had wings of skin, just like bats—and so, just like dragons! But they weren't dinosaurs and they didn't breathe fire.

Other kinds of reptiles lived in the sea and looked like dolphins. Or like the Loch Ness monster. Who knows, perhaps that monster is real—some people think so.

Dinosaurs laid eggs. Delicious for breakfast!

Cat turns up.

Suddenly she's there in the forest,
right near Wolf's house. Wolf is scared
sick. He's terrified of Cat, but he doesn't
show it.

"Dog's here. You know, my cousin.
He's on guard and he'll bark you away!"
he warns.

Huh. Dog's not barking. He's fast
asleep!

Cat looks at Dog. He's snoring loudly
and his belly moves up and down.

"Is that really your cousin?" asks Cat.
"Dog's white, isn't he?"

"Dog was digging a hole," Wolf
explains. "He got all dirty."

"I see," says Cat, licking her coat.

She stretches and yawns. She glances
at the hole, and casts another glance at
Dog. She says, "That can't really be Dog.

But thanks to your clue I know what
sort of animal it is. It's black and digs
deep underground. Your cousin is
a mole, Wolf!"

Cat laughs loudly.

Wolf gets angry. He snarls, "Get out, Cat!
You don't know what you're talking about.

Dog is a dog. He was hunting for treasure but he found a bone as hard as stone. There it is, right next to Dog."

Cat gives him a funny look. "A bone. That's a bone? I thought it was a tree. It's as thick as a tree trunk and twice your height."

Wolf nods. "It's a dinosaur's bone. It's very, very old."

Cat purrs. She has a plan. She gives a fake laugh.

Wolf doesn't notice.

"That bone isn't from a dinosaur. It's a dragon's bone," she says.

"But Dog said..." says Wolf.

"Dog's lying!" Cat hisses. "There's treasure in the ground. You said so yourself!"

Wolf scratches his head. He takes the map and looks at the X. It's right in front of his door, where there's now a hole. Is the treasure still in there? But the hole's already so deep!

Cat sidles up to Wolf. Right next to him! Wolf trembles.

Cat says hoarsely, "There was once a dragon's nest here in this forest, right beside your house. The dragon slept deep in an underground cave. On a mountain of gold. That's what dragons do. That gold is the treasure.

"But Dog doesn't want you to find it. Look for it yourself, Wolf. Dig more holes. Root up trees! Rip out bushes! Seek until you find!" Cat hisses at Wolf.

Wolf freezes with fear.

Cat likes that! She hisses again, for the fun of it. Then she turns around and is gone.

TRY THIS

Treasure chest Take an empty drink carton. Draw a line around the middle. Draw arches above this line on the two narrow sides to make a shape for your lid to curve over. Leaving the back of the carton as it is, cut away the upper part of the carton at the sides, following your curved lines. Cut away the top of the carton at the front by following your straight line. Now bend the back over the curved sides to the front of the carton and fasten. Decorate. Fill your treasure chest with chocolate money and a candy necklace.

Done!

In fairy tales, a dragon guards a princess in a tower. The princess has to be rescued by a gallant prince, or a bold knight. He slays the dragon then marries the princess. She becomes his treasure! And they live happily ever after.

rockets
and the
moon

Dog wakes up. It's already night!

Where am I? he wonders as he looks around.

He's not at home, or at Wolf's place. He can't see any forest or trees. The land is completely bare. But Wolf's house is still there. How can that be?

I'm dreaming, thinks Dog. I must be dreaming of the moon, because the moon's exactly like this. Nothing grows there.

Dog often looks at the moon and wishes he could go there. And now his dream has come true. In a dream!

But hey, what's that? Dog can see the moon, there in the sky.

How can that be? Dog is on the moon and he can see the moon. There's only one moon, isn't there?

"This dream makes no sense," Dog calls out. "Or is it not really a dream? Am I not asleep? Am I wandering around in Wolf's forest? But where's the forest? And where's Wolf?"

"Ahh-woooooooo!" Dog hears.

That's Wolf howling. It sounds loud at night. Cat will hear it soon and she'll turn up. And tease Wolf!

"I'm coming!" calls Dog. "As quick as I can. Hold on, I'll save you! Where are you?"

"Here in the hole!" Wolf howls.

That's no help to Dog. There's more than one hole. There might be ten or eleven. Or twelve! It looks exactly like the moon.

"Ahh-woooooooo!" Wolf's still howling.

Dog listens carefully and works out where Wolf's voice is coming from. Sure enough, he finds him, deep down in a hole.

"It's Cat's fault," bawls Wolf. "She told me there was treasure in my forest. The dragon's treasure. So I dug and I dug."

"What about your forest?" asks Dog. "Where's it gone?"

"It went ahh–waaaaaay!" wails Wolf. "Tree by tree and bush by bush. And I still haven't found the treasure!"

Dog says no more. He feels very sorry for Wolf. And very sorry for the forest. If only it had been a dream!

"I wish Cat would take off to the moon," growls Dog. And he means it.

Earth is a planet. It orbits the sun, but not alone. Seven other planets also circle the sun: Mercury, Venus, Mars, Jupiter, Saturn, Uranus, and Neptune. Together they make up our solar system. The sun in the middle is our star. There are many trillions of stars in the universe, and numerous planets, too.

Stars and planets are celestial bodies. The moon is a celestial body too, because like a planet or a star it's a sphere, or ball, in space. But the moon does not circle the sun. It orbits Earth. That's why it's a moon rather than a planet. We have only one moon, which is why it's usually called "the moon." Mars has two moons and Jupiter has sixty-seven!

The universe takes up lots of space.

QUIZ

What is a celestial body?

A   An angel in heaven

B   A person in space

C   A sphere in space

Does the moon have a face? It looks as if it does. There are dark patches on the moon called "maria." "Mare" is Latin for sea, "maria" for seas. But there's no water on the moon. And so there are no real seas either. The "maria" are flat areas formed by old volcanic eruptions. The lunar surface also has many craters where it has been hit by space debris.

Have you ever seen "shooting stars"? They're really meteors: fiery fragments of space debris. Most debris from outer space burns up as soon as it enters Earth's atmosphere, the layer of air around the planet.

That's a rock, not a star!

Sometimes a meteor is so big that it hits Earth before it has time to burn up. Then the meteor is called a meteorite. A large meteorite can create an enormous crater on Earth. That happened once 65 million years ago before people lived on Earth, in the time of the dinosaurs. The impact created a series of natural catastrophes. These days, most scientists think that the dinosaurs—and a lot of other animals and plants—were wiped out by that meteorite.

Around the moon there is no atmosphere as there is on Earth. That's why even the smallest piece of space debris can hit the moon without burning up.

Long ago, meteorites damaged the moon's surface and lava flowed out from inside the moon. That explains how a "mare" is a sea, not of water, but of cooled volcanic rock.

Nothing grows on the moon. The lunar landscape is bare and barren.

QUIZ

What is a lunar landscape?

A   A landscape seen by moonlight

B   A bare surface covered in craters

C   A moon landing

Wolf is hard at work.

Yes, really! He's even singing as he hammers and saws.

"My racket will be ready soon.
It will fly up to the moon.
It has lots and lots of room.
For Cat to...um...ah..."

Wolf stops singing to hunt for a word. A word that rhymes with oom! But he can't think of one.

Dog arrives. "What are you up to?" he asks.

"I'm making a racket," says Wolf proudly. "Your wish is about to come true!"

Dog looks puzzled. "My wish? What wish?"

Wolf sighs. His good mood disappears.

He growls, "You made a wish, didn't you? You said:

I wish Cat would take off to the moon.

And you know what? That's my wish, too, so I'm doing something about it. Go and catch Cat, Dog, while I'll carry on with this. The racket's almost ready."

Dog bursts out laughing. "You don't mean racket. You mean rocket!"

Wolf blushes. "What does it matter," he snarls. "This word or that! As long as the thing flies far and high. Hurry up, Dog. Catch that beast. It's time we got rid of her."

Dog sighs. "I won't do it, Wolf. I don't feel like catching Cat. The moon is much too far away. You can't get there."

"Of course you can!" cries Wolf. "I saw it in a book. One of your books, Dog. A man was walking on the moon."

Dog nods. "That's true. A man did walk on the moon."

"And once there was a dog who flew in a rocket."

"So it can be done!" says Wolf.

Dog nods again and laughs: "It's true, a rocket goes a long way. But a racket like yours won't bc going anywhere!"

More than half a century ago, the Americans and Russians were in competition. Both wanted to reach the moon. From there, they could keep a better eye on each other. But who would be first? An astronaut or a cosmonaut?

An astronaut is a "star-sailor." "Astronaut" comes from the Greek words "astron" meaning "star" and "nautes" meaning "sailor." The Americans invented the name. The Russians had "cosmonauts," not "astronauts." "Kosmos" is ancient Greek for the universe or outer space. So a cosmonaut is a "space-sailor."

A taikonaut is a Chinese space explorer. "Taikong" is Cantonese for "universe."

One dreams of the stars and the other of space, but in the end they do exactly the same thing.

A space voyager without a rocket is like a cyclist without a bicycle. They get nowhere.

The first rocket into space came from Russia. It carried no crew, nor did it land on the moon. Instead, it carried *Sputnik 1*, a satellite. The Sputnik was itself a moon— an artificial moon, because it orbited Earth.

Sputnik 2 had a passenger.
A small, brave dog called Laika.
She died within an hour or two
from heat and fear. Poor Laika!

The Americans did better than the
Russians. They succeeded in putting
the first people on the moon. The
first footprint in moon dust was
made by Neil Armstrong.
He said these famous words:

*That's one small step
for a man,
one giant leap
for mankind.*

Laika was a stray dog from Moscow. Her name in Russian meant "barker."

QUIZ

What is an astronaut?

A An American space voyager

B A Russian space voyager

C A Chinese space voyager

TRY THIS

Papier-mâché rocket Take an empty drink bottle. Cut three rocket wings out of cardboard. Attach them to the lower half of the bottle with wide tape. Rip up small pieces of paper and glue these all over the rocket. Leave to dry overnight, then paint.

Done!

Cat's leaving very soon! I'll shoot her to the moon!

A rocket is very fast. Faster than the fastest car. Faster than the fastest plane. Faster than the fastest high-speed train.

Why does a rocket have to fly fast? To get to the moon on time? Hardly! The moon will wait. The rocket flies as fast as it does in order to escape Earth's pull. Because Earth is so large, it has very strong gravity, which attracts everything near it. The chair you're sitting on, the table, this book, and you as well: all are pulled by Earth's gravity. Without gravity you'd be floating in space, just like an astronaut in the universe. A rocket is also attracted to Earth. Only with very powerful engines can it tear itself free of gravity. Because of space travel, we can communicate around the planet, by phone, radio, and television. For these we need satellites. A satellite is an artificial moon, like *Sputnik*. Many satellites circle the Earth. Happily they no longer have dogs in them. They have no crew either.

Signals are sent from Earth to satellites. The satellites bounce the signals back to other points on Earth. If you phone a friend, the message sometimes goes out into space before they receive it!

Wolf sulks. He didn't find any treasure. His forest is dead. And his racket isn't a rocket.

"Chin up," says Dog. "Your forest will grow again. Plant a tree here, a tree there. An oak, a birch, a beech. A spruce or a fir. An alder and an elm. And how about a willow? That will grow fast. I'll help you, Wolf. I'm your cousin, after all."

That's true. Dog is kind and loyal. Look,
he's made a start already, dragging a
bush to a hole. It's a perfect fit.

"Ha," laughs Dog. "Doesn't it look
good here?"

"Hm…" growls Wolf.

Dog is so busy. Doesn't he ever stop?

Dog knows everything and does
everything.

As for Wolf, he does nothing.

He knows nothing either, which
makes him feel useless.

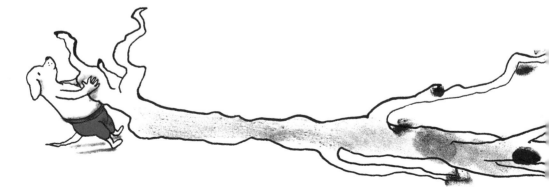

But hang on… There's one thing Wolf knows. He laughs and looks at Dog as he makes up a rhyme:

> *"Dog is my cousin*
> *Each day of the year*
> *No matter what happens*
> *He'll always be there."*

And now Wolf does something too. Can you guess what? He takes a nap.

And that's not nothing!

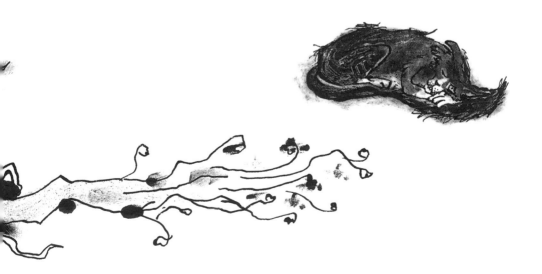

ANSWERS TO THE QUIZZES

10	**C**	54	**B**	92 above	**B**
15	**B**	57	**B**	92 below	**A**
21	**B**	68	**C**	109	**C**
27	**A**	69	**A**	111	**B**
39	**C**	80	**B**	117	**A**
46	**C**	87	**C**		

This edition first published in 2016 by Gecko Press
PO Box 9335, Marion Square, Wellington 6141, New Zealand
info@geckopress.com

English language edition © Gecko Press Ltd 2016

First American edition published in 2016 by Gecko Press USA,
an imprint of Gecko Press Ltd

2014 © Uitgeverij Lannoo nv. For the original edition.
Original title: *Hond weet alles en Wolf niets*. Translated from the
Dutch language. www.lannoo.com

Distributed in the United States and Canada by Lerner Publishing Group,
www.lernerbooks.com
Distributed in the United Kingdom by Bounce Sales and Marketing,
www.bouncemarketing.co.uk
Distributed in Australia by Scholastic Australia,
www.scholastic.com.au
Distributed in New Zealand by Upstart Distribution,
www.upstartpress.co.nz

The publisher gratefully acknowledges the support of the Dutch
Foundation for Literature.

N ederlands
letterenfonds
dutch foundation
for literature

The translation of this book was funded by the Flemish Literature Fund.
www.flemishliterature.be

Vlaams
Fonds
voor de
Letteren

Cover design by Spencer Levine
Edited by Penelope Todd
Typesetting by Vida & Luke Kelly, New Zealand
Printed in China by Everbest Printing Co. Ltd,
an accredited ISO 14001 & FSC certified printer

Hardback ISBN: 978-1-776570-36-2
Paperback ISBN: 978-1-776570-37-9
Ebook available

For more curiously good books,
visit www.geckopress.com